MURDER IN THE VILLA

A MAGGIE NEWBERRY HALLOWEEN NOVELLA

SUSAN KIERNAN-LEWIS

SAN MARCO PRESS

It was a dark and spooky Halloween night in Provence...

Maggie and Laurent embark on a chilling adventure when their car breaks down on their way to a village Halloween party. Dressed as French Resistance Fighters, the pair take refuge from the coming storm in an old villa set far back from the road where they meet an old woman who thinks the war is still going on. Believing them to be fellow Resistance fighters like herself, Valène Lavallière reveals her tragic story of forbidden love and a heart-stopping secret from nearly eighty ago. As the storm builds outside, Maggie and Laurent soon realize that not everything they are seeing is the truth and the secrets that the old woman harbors could very well make the morning after this Halloween night one they never live to see.

Death by Cliché
Dying to be French
Ménage à Murder
Killing it in Paris
Murder Flambé
Deadly Faux Pas
Toujours Dead
Murder in the Christmas Market
Deadly Adieu
Murdering Madeleine
Murder Carte Blanche
Death à la Drumstick

The Savannah Time Travel Mysteries
Killing Time in Georgia
Scarlett Must Die

The Stranded in Provence Mysteries
Parlez-Vous Murder?
Crime and Croissants
Accent on Murder
A Bad Éclair Day
Croak, Monsieur!
Death du Jour
Murder Très Gauche
Wined and Died
Murder, Voila!
A French Country Christmas
Fromage to Eternity

The Irish End Games
Free Falling
Going Gone

Heading Home
Blind Sided
Rising Tides
Cold Comfort
Never Never
Wit's End
Dead On
White Out
Black Out
End Game

1

Something Old, Something New

Maggie dabbed at her lips and squinted in the bathroom mirror. The lipstick was much redder than she normally wore. Her dark hair, usually worn straight to her shoulders, was caught up in a nineteen forties velvet snood.

I should wear this thing more often, she thought as she tilted her head to get a good view from every side in the mirror. The snood helped tame her frizz while still framing her face. She stepped back from the mirror to eye her costume, a dress in a small floral pattern against a dark background that any woman in the forties might have worn. It clung to her curves and hit her just below the knee.

"Did women really dress that sexy in the forties?"

Maggie turned to glance at her husband Laurent who was eying her from the bedroom door. He wore the unmistakably rakish ensemble of a French Resistance fighter, complete with leather jacket and beret. He'd been grumpy about it, but Maggie had insisted that the costume party they were headed to tonight would be fun.

"I'll take that as a compliment," she said, putting her hand coquettishly on one hip.

"We could skip the party," he suggested with an arched eyebrow.

"After going to all the trouble of getting a sitter?" she responded with mock horror. "No way am I wasting an evening out."

"Perhaps it wouldn't be wasted."

She walked over to him and raised up on tiptoe to kiss him on the cheek.

"You just don't want to go," she said.

"*Exactement.*"

His hand clasped her by the waist and drew her to him.

"No, now none of that," she admonished as she slipped out of his embrace. "Grace says we're always late and I mean to prove her wrong tonight."

He snorted in response. A handsome, broad-shouldered man with dark, nearly pupil-less eyes, Laurent stood well over six foot five—unusually tall for a Frenchman.

"You do know that Halloween doesn't exist in France," he said as he followed her downstairs.

"Of course it exists," Maggie said. "You guys just don't observe it."

Maggie found herself more than a little relieved that trick or treating wasn't a tradition in France since Amelie—a handful even at six—would no doubt be even more interested in the *tricking* part.

Maggie stopped and collected her cardigan and purse from a wooden bench at the bottom of the stairs. She glanced around the foyer and into the living room. It was so quiet in the house without Amelie and the dogs rampaging through it that it felt surreal. When Danielle had come to collect Amelie for the night, she'd insisted on taking the two dogs too. It almost felt like the days before Maggie and Laurent had children.

Outside the light had already faded to grey. Maggie thought it seemed to get dark sooner in Provence than just about any place else on the planet. She debated bringing a coat—it was chilly out—but decided against it. She didn't want to ruin the effect of her outfit with a jacket from L. L. Bean. Just then her cellphone rang, and she pulled it out of her purse. She could see by the caller identification screen that it was her best friend Grace calling.

"Hey," Maggie said, answering. "We're just leaving."

"What did you decide to go as?"

Grace had been Maggie's best friend since the two met well over twenty years ago in France. Today, Grace managed a bed and breakfast owned by Laurent, and lived there with her grandson Philippe, Danielle, and an assortment of dogs and cats.

"Laurent is going as a Resistance fighter." Maggie said.

"How in the world did you talk him into that?"

"It wasn't easy. And I'm going as a typical forties housewife. So we match. How about you?"

"I decided to go the scary route this year."

"Are we talking Martha Stewart in a bathing suit?"

"Ha ha, darling. No, I'm going as a sexy witch."

"You always go as a sexy witch."

"That's because it works for me."

Grace had recently become single again. With a full-time business to run, a grandson to raise in a foreign country, and turning fifty, she'd had to realize that the dating game was played differently now. Maggie had spent many an evening listening to her recent romantic laments. Even at fifty Grace was still stunningly beautiful. But age catches up with us all, Maggie noted. Even goddesses.

As beautiful as Grace was, she wasn't twenty. And even in France, twenty was better.

"Maggie," Laurent said impatiently from the front door where he stood tossing car keys in his hand.

"Gotta go," Maggie said to Grace. "My sexy French hero is calling me. See you there."

2

A Dark & Stormy Night

The night air was crisp and cool with a hint of frost. As Maggie slid into the passenger's seat, she couldn't help but think that on this Halloween night more than any other, the world seemed rife with a sense of mystery that was almost tangible.

Growing up back in Atlanta, she and her brother and sister would walk their upscale Buckhead neighborhood on Halloween night and return home with bulging sacks of candy. Passing her friends on the residential streets had always been an especially fun part of the night—a night where they were allowed to wander the streets without parental supervision.

When Maggie became a parent herself, she remembered noting on more than one occasion how glad she was that allowing Jemmy and Mila to wander the streets to knock on strangers' doors wasn't something she had to worry about.

Laurent drove down the long winding driveway of their

mas, Domaine St-Buvard. Laurent had inherited the property twenty-five years ago from a bachelor uncle he never knew. Since then, he and Maggie had raised three children and created a prosperous vineyard property.

Maggie had heard there was a possibility of rain tonight. The sky was dark and foreboding with heavy clouds overhead. As they drove, she watched the trees lining the road form a black tunnel. As usual this time of year, it felt as if the whole world was in a state of transition, preparing for the coming winter ahead.

"Grace said she's going as a sexy witch," Maggie said as Laurent turned onto an access road heading in the direction of Aix—a good twenty-five kilometers away.

"I will never understand any part of this tradition," he said.

"I guess you had to grow up with it. In the US, you grow up dressing as a Disney character to gradually being too old for trick-or- treating to finally going to Halloween parties dressed as a sexy hooker."

"I repeat."

Maggie leaned over and squeezed his arm.

"Thanks for being a good sport. I'm really looking forward to tonight."

Laurent only snorted but Maggie knew he was pleased that his effort had made her happy.

"You know this is supposed to be the spookiest night of the year," she said as she watched the passing scenery. "Graves open up and ghosts and goblins come out to play."

He snorted again and this time she was able to interpret it as playful disdain.

"Obviously I don't believe in all that," she said. "But it's fun to get spooked, don't you think? To tell ghost stories by the fire and get chills?"

"I have never understood this desire to scare yourself."

Maggie knew that Laurent's childhood had been a hard one with very few if any campfires to sit around. And later in his life, the idea of deliberately scaring himself would have seemed insane to him—not when his occupation as a professional thief was a high-wire act played without a net almost every single day of his life.

"Did you talk to Luc today?" she asked.

Luc was their adopted son who had moved to California six years ago for school, had fallen in love with both the country and a girl, and had decided to stay. His decision had disappointed Laurent who had been counting on him coming back to help run the family vineyard. However, Maggie knew that time eventually sapped the sharpness out of every bitter pill, and more than his disappointment, Laurent wanted Luc to be happy.

"He said he wants to marry in California because of her family," Laurent said.

"Well, that's understandable, right?" Maggie asked. "I mean, I wish they'd marry here but I do see why she would prefer her own home."

Laurent shrugged. Maggie knew he wasn't happy about Luc's decision not to marry at Domaine St-Buvard. But he would accept it. Eventually.

She turned to watch the trees fly by, casting eerie shadows on the road. The moon was hiding behind heavy clouds.

"Why did we go this way?" she asked. "It's practically deserted."

"It connects to an ancillary road," Laurent said. "Or at least it used to."

Maggie brushed aside a moment of pique produced by Laurent's decision to try a new route on a night when she was determined not to be late. She held her tongue though. He'd already committed to the route and turning around now would only take more time. At one point, she thought she saw a glimmer of light flickering through the trees from a house set way back from the road.

Otherwise, the only light around them came from the headlights of their car, which cast a dim glow into the mist that lingered over the road and surrounding fields. Maggie had to admit that everything looked fittingly ghostly. She found herself rubbing the goosebumps off her arms.

Suddenly, the car began to cough and sputter. Maggie glanced at Laurent and saw he was frowning.

"Laurent?" she said.

"It's fine," he said seconds before a strange grinding noise emanated from the engine. The car slowed.

"Are we stopping?" she asked, her voice rising.

"Well, not deliberately," he said.

Maggie braced her hands against the dashboard as the car slowed until it finally came to a stop on the shoulder of the road.

They sat in the darkness for a few moments. Laurent turned the ignition and swore.

"Laurent?" Maggie asked again. "Is it petrol? Did we run out?"

"We did not run out of petrol," he said between gritted teeth as he opened the door and stepped out. Maggie watched him open the car hood, using the light from his cellphone to see by. She heard him cursing again. She couldn't wait inside another moment and quickly got out of the car to join him outside as he peered under the hood.

"What is it?" she asked.

He didn't answer and Maggie turned to look around,

suddenly realizing how isolated they were. She found herself shivering against the chill in the air as it drilled relentlessly through her thin cotton sweater.

3

___

Any Port in a Storm

The air felt thick and heavy around her as Maggie stood on the side of the road. Overhead, the clouds were dark and ominous, roiling and churning like a cauldron. She remembered the weather report and pulled her sweater tighter around her. The wind seemed to pick up, whipping through the trees and bending the grass around them where they stood on the side of the road. The air felt charged with electricity.

"We'll need a tow," Laurent said, as he closed the hood.

"Are you serious?" Maggie said, her feeling of panic and disappointment merging together and making her sound shriller than she'd intended.

Grace was probably already at the party, she thought. Maggie imagined the music was probably in full swing— and the dancing—Laurent had promised he'd dance with her tonight. She felt her heart sink into her stomach. She'd been looking forward to this night all week.

Maybe they could get an Uber to come out?

Maggie pulled out her cellphone and instantly saw she had no service. She looked at Laurent and saw he was looking at his own phone. She felt a flinch of annoyance at him. If he hadn't taken this stupid short cut they would at least have cell service when their car stalled!

"So what now?" she asked briskly.

"Let's get it off the road," Laurent said. "We don't want to get hit from behind."

He opened the driver's side door and put the car in neutral. Maggie got into the driver's seat and steered it while Laurent pushed it off the road. By the time they finished, the first drops of rain had started to fall. Maggie shivered in the car as Laurent got inside next to her in the passenger's seat.

"Do we just wait here?" she asked and realized then that they hadn't seen a single other car on the road since they'd pulled onto it.

"There was a house about a mile back," Laurent said. "You stay here and I'll—"

"Are you crazy?" Maggie said at the same time a flash of lightning lit up the sky, revealing black spikes of branches on the trees that hugged the road. The rain fell harder, pounding against the car roof like a drumbeat.

"I'm going with you," she said firmly.

"Maggie, you will get wet," Laurent said reasonably.

"I don't care. I'm not staying out here alone."

He laughed. "Afraid of the graves opening up?"

"That's not funny," she said sharply.

"Fine," he said, shrugging out of his leather jacket and draping it over her shoulders. "But we must run."

They each flung open their car doors and stepped out into the rain. It wasn't too bad yet, Maggie decided. But with the sporadic flashes of lightning, she knew it was going to get worse. If they could make it to that house they'd seen, they could dry off, call an Uber—or maybe get Grace to come and get them—and be at the party within the hour.

Laurent grabbed her hand, and they ran down the highway back the way they'd come. Within minutes, their clothes were soaked through, and their hair plastered to their faces. The rain was coming down in sheets, obscuring their vision and making any run on the slick road treacherous.

As she ran, Maggie heard thunder in the near distance which added to her sense of urgency. But it also added to a feeling she realized had developed deep in her gut that she could not shake.

A feeling that seemed to be telling her something bad was about to happen.

4

The Devil's Playground

The house they'd seen earlier was set far back from the road. As Maggie and Laurent stood at the end of its driveway—a single dirt and gravel road nearly obscured by a tangle of overgrown shrubbery—Maggie could barely make out the house set on a hill, surrounded by woods. Even from fifty yards away, the house was an imposing stone structure, with tall front windows and a peaked roof that seemed to reach up to the sky.

More than a house or even a *mas*, Maggie thought, this was a bonafide villa. Its dark silhouette awakened something unpleasant in her gut.

As they drew closer, the windows looked like blackened eyes staring out at the world. The villa's long, sagging roof drooped over a stone balcony as if threatening to collapse at any moment. Even as miserable, cold and wet as Maggie was, few things in her life had ever looked less inviting to her.

"Maybe we should keep walking," she said, stopping.

Laurent turned to look at Maggie. He wiped the rain from his face.

"Why are you stopping?" he shouted. "It's just there!"

Maggie was astonished that Laurent wasn't having the same reaction she was—a visceral reaction that said in no uncertain terms *stay away*. But with the rain pouring down, she knew this was not the moment to attempt to explain her gut reaction to him. She took a breath to steady herself and reached for his hand. Instantly, he pulled her down the driveway until they reached the front verandah.

The entrance was framed by a pair of stone pillars that were crumbling and barely holding up the roof. From the lintel above was a pair of chipped and damaged gargoyles leering down at them.

Every fiber of Maggie's body told her not to go inside. She wanted to tell Laurent that they should go back to the car—even if it meant spending the night there. But he was already pulling her onto the veranda. She felt the wood sag under her weight when she stepped onto it. The rain was harder now and the wind was rattling the loose shutters of the main floor windows.

"Laurent, there's nobody home!" she shouted over the din of the wind and the rain, suddenly desperate to convince him to leave.

"It is shelter!" he said, pulling her forward.

Once on the threshold he dropped her hand and banged on the large wooden door with his fist. Maggie closed her eyes to blot out the creepy facade. And it was then that she noticed the smell. Even in the rain, the breeze seemed to carry the odor of mold and mildew to her. And something else undefinable.

She felt Laurent's hand snake around her waist and pull her close to him. She didn't know if he did it because he too was feeling wary about the place or because he saw how cold she was. Before she could decide which, she saw a glimmer of light peeked out from one of the sidelights of the front door.

Someone is home.

Who would live in such a place? Maggie was more unnerved than she had been when just a minute before she thought it was abandoned. The door opened slowly and before them stood an old woman holding a kerosene lantern.

At first Maggie thought she was an apparition. She wore a long cream-colored gown and her white hair seemed to float around her shoulders.

Laurent, nearly drowned out by the sound of the storm, spoke in fast French to her. The old woman looked up at the sky and then beckoned them inside.

5

Time Tripping

The room Maggie and Laurent stepped into was a time capsule from a bygone era. Maggie looked around in amazement. It was filled with antique furniture and lit by a few flickering candles which cast dancing shadows on the walls.

The old woman led them to a large parlor where a weak fire burned in the hearth. Maggie was surprised they hadn't seen the smoke from the chimney. The only furniture in the room was an old armchair beneath the window, its cushions stained and threadbare. Past the parlor Maggie could see the bare-bones dining room which contained only a rough wooden table and a single chair.

Aside from the smell of the fire burning in the fireplace, the air was thick with the scent of old wood, but also something much less pleasant that Maggie couldn't put her finger on. She listened to the wind whistle through the holes in the stonework, causing the brick and plaster to rub together like sandpaper.

Maggie had the strongest feeling that these walls held long-forgotten stories and secrets.

None of them good.

"Please come sit," the old woman said.

She was a small woman, her face etched with wrinkles. Despite her apparent frailty, Maggie thought she projected an air of dignity, as if she carried a legacy of pain and suffering from someone who had seen the worst of humanity.

"I am Valène Lavallière," the woman said. "You are both welcome."

"Thank you," Laurent said. "Our car broke down. If we could use your telephone, we will call our friends and be on our way."

"I apologize but I have no phone," Madame Lavallière said.

Looking around the room, that didn't surprise Maggie. The whole room felt like it was from another time. No electric lights, no phone, nothing that would mark it as any different from one in the nineteen hundreds. Even Madame Lavallière herself was dressed in a basic dress that could have been worn in the early nineteen hundreds.

"My dear," Madame Lavallière said to Maggie, "you must change into dry clothes."

In spite of the heat emanating from the fireplace, Maggie was shivering in her soaking clothes. She looked at Laurent who appeared to be trying to decide what their next move was now that there was no telephone.

"A towel would be helpful," Maggie said to the old woman, moving closer to the fireplace.

"Nonsense, my dear. I have clothing for you. I am prepared."

Maggie thought that was a strange thing to say, but in any event she knew she couldn't stay in her wet clothes.

"That would be great," she said.

"Come with me to the kitchen," Madame Lavallière said. "The clothes are there and I will make tea."

Maggie followed her through the dining room and into the kitchen, feeling her feet squish inside her shoes.

Like the parlor, the kitchen was large and Maggie imagined that at one time it must have been a hub of warmth and the family center. But now it was just big and empty. Its floors were dull and scarred and the peeling paint on the walls revealed patches of bare plaster beneath. A large, iron stove that Maggie imagined had once radiated warmth and homey aromas was now cold. In spite of that, she could detect the scent of just-baked bread. She put her hand on the stove to confirm to herself that it hadn't been used—probably in decades.

In the middle of the room sat a sturdy oak table, its surface etched with the marks of countless meals and conversations. Around it was positioned three mismatched chairs. Like the rest of the house, the room felt as if it had been trapped in a time warp. Even though it was cold and seemingly unused now, it was easy to see how it once had served its family before life had been interrupted by the war.

"Here you are," Madame Lavallière said going to a cupboard at the back of the kitchen.

She pulled out a stack of men's trousers, a shirt and a thick wool sweater. All the clothes were from the nineteen-forties. There could be no doubt about that. Maggie imagined that these must be clothes from Madame Lavallière's family. She took the stack in her hands.

"There is a back room where you may change," Madame Lavallière said.

Maggie went into the room and quickly stripped off her wet dress, as well as the hose on which she'd painted a line up the back of her leg to look more time appropriate. She draped her now soggy sweater on the back of a chair and pulled on the dry pants and shirt Madame Lavallière had given her. There was a leather belt too and socks. Maggie left her shoes on the floor close to where she hung her wet clothes and pulled on the thick socks. She didn't imagine she or Laurent were going anywhere anytime soon. She could live the next hour or so in her stockinged feet.

When she joined Laurent and Madame Lavallière in the living room, Laurent instantly stood up and frowned when he saw her outfit.

"It's warm," Maggie said before he could comment. "And dry. You should try it."

"Yes, of course," Madame Lavallière said. "I have men's clothing for you too, Monsieur." She eyed him critically. "Although you are very big, and I am afraid nothing would fit."

"That's all right," Laurent said. "We can't stay long anyway."

Madame Lavallière sat back down and began to pour the tea. Maggie noted there were no cookies or bread. She was sure she'd smelled fresh bread. Madame Lavallière handed her a cup of tea and Maggie gratefully warmed her hands around the cup.

"Are the *boche* after you?" the old woman asked, her face frowning in concern.

Maggie wasn't sure she'd heard correctly.

"Who?" she asked.

The woman looked instantly suspicious.

"Did I make a mistake?" She pointed to Laurent. "He is with the Resistance, no? I thought for sure..."

Maggie realized that the old woman was confused.

She thinks the war is still going on!

"We are in costume for a party," Laurent said.

Madame Lavallière looked at him and narrowed her eyes.

"What are you saying?" she said. "Are you working for the Germans? Who are you?"

Her voice was suddenly shrill.

"You didn't make a mistake," Maggie said hurriedly. "He *is* with the Resistance."

She ignored the surprised look Laurent shot her. Madame Lavallière seemed to relax a bit.

"Have you come for the pilot?" she asked. "I am afraid he is not here anymore."

"No, we're meeting in the woods," Maggie said. "And we got caught in the storm."

But Madame Lavallière was once more looking at her with suspicion.

"You are married?" she asked arching an eyebrow at Maggie.

"We are," Maggie said. "And yourself? Is there a Monsieur Lavallière at home?"

The old woman hesitated but then seemed to have made a decision about something. She poured her tea.

"My husband is in a prisoner of war camp," she said. "Daily I pray he is fed and healthy."

"I'm sure," Maggie said, but her brain was doing the calculation and it did not add up.

Even if Madame Lavallière was in her nineties—which she easily looked to be—she would still have been too young to have had a husband in 1944. Maggie wasn't going to question her. The old woman was clearly confused about what time it was and it wouldn't help things to point out any errors to her. She was about to take a sip of her tea when a shadow moved past the window behind Madame Lavallière. Realizing it wasn't likely that anyone was outside in this storm, Maggie quickly dismissed what she'd seen as a trick of the night sky.

As they sat and drank their tea, Maggie heard the faint ticking of an old grandfather clock which echoed through the room. Despite the storm outside, there was an eerie stillness to the room.

Turning to look at Laurent, Maggie could tell he was uneasy—whether by her lies or the woman or the house itself. And because of his gift for always knowing when trouble was coming and how to deal with it, seeing his uneasiness was enough to make Maggie very uneasy.

6

Poisoning the Well

As the storm continued to rage, Maggie thought the lightning strikes seemed to be getting closer and closer. She felt a tension developing in her chest. She turned to Laurent.

"So what's the plan?" she asked. "No phone, pouring down rain. What do you think?"

"I'm thinking," Laurent said with a frown.

"I will find you a sweater, Monsieur," Madame Lavallière said to him. "An Allied pilot left it last month. I meant to burn it, but it will serve you tonight I think."

Laurent thanked her as the old woman got up and went back into the kitchen.

"What are you doing?" Laurent said to Maggie.

"She thinks it's still the war," Maggie said. "I'm just playing along. What does it hurt? I think it would only confuse her to try to explain why we're dressed like this."

"I don't like it," he said plucking his wet shirt away from his chest and frowning deeply.

"Monsieur?"

Madame Lavallière came back into the room with a dry shirt and a sweater for him. "I think these may fit. You are very big."

"*Merci*, Madame Lavallière," Laurent said, quickly stripping off his shirt in front of the fire and pulling on the sweater.

Maggie turned to Madame Lavallière.

"Do you live here alone?" she asked.

The woman tilted her head as if looking at Maggie in a new light. A veil of hardness seemed to drop over her expression.

"I wait for my husband's return," she said.

She narrowed her eyes at Maggie.

"Do you not have children?"

"We do," Maggie said. "But they're not here. We sent them to America."

Maggie heard Laurent groan. She knew she was offering up too many lies and even a confused old woman might be able to see the holes in them.

"Your children are in America? Are you Jewish?" Madame Lavallière looked surprised and glanced at both of them as if trying to determine if they might be.

"What? No," Maggie said. "I'm American so our children went there to further their education. They're all grown up."

"I see."

But the old woman was still frowning. She was clearly not happy with what Maggie was telling her.

"How did an American woman come to join the Resistance?" Madame Lavallière asked.

"Well, I'm a part of the Allied advance," Maggie said as she caught Laurent rolling his eyes. "And I wanted to be near my husband." She put a hand on his knee and pinched him.

"I see," Madame Lavallière said. "Of course, a woman would want to be near her husband no matter the world situation."

After that, and mostly to distract her, Maggie asked her about the history of the villa.

"My parents and my grandparents owned it," Madame Lavallière said. "I have lived here all my life."

Maggie gave Laurent a pointed look since he tended to know most of the history of the area, but he only shrugged as if to say he didn't know this one.

"When was your husband taken captive?" Maggie asked.

"What are you talking about, Madame? My husband lives with me," Madame Lavallière said, frowning at Maggie once more.

"Oh! I'm sorry," Maggie said, flustered. "I misunder-stood. Do you have children?"

"Why are you asking me these questions? Who do you really work for?"

Maggie looked helplessly at Laurent who gave her a *are-you-happy-now?* look.

"Did the Gestapo send you?" Madame Lavallière said standing up, her lips and chin trembling.

"No, of course not! Would...would a German agent speak French as well as my husband does?"

Madame Lavallière looked mistrustingly at Laurent.

"He would if he was a double agent," she said.

"He's not a double agent," Maggie said. "He loves his country. He would never betray it."

"People do," Madame Lavallière said. "People do all manner of terrible things."

Maggie didn't have an answer for that, and she did think

that very possibly she was making things worse by pretending the time was still wartime, so she said nothing. After a moment, Madame Lavallière stood up.

"Where are my manners? You must be hungry. I have some goat cheese in the larder."

She got up and went back to the kitchen.

"Will you stop now?" Laurent said, in a scolding tone. "You are making things worse. You are making her more confused."

Just then a long creak sounded from overhead. It was unmistakably as if someone had stepped on a loose board.

"What was that?" Maggie asked in a low whisper.

Laurent didn't answer. He was staring overhead at the spot where the noise had come. That in itself unnerved Maggie even more than hearing the noise. It meant he didn't have an answer for what they'd just heard.

"I'll check it out," Laurent said, standing up.

Maggie grabbed his arm.

"Laurent, no!" she hissed. "You don't know what's up there!"

"Ghosts, *chérie*?" he said, giving her a half smile. "I will deal with them. Meanwhile, tell her I've gone to look for the toilet."

Maggie watched helplessly as he walked soundlessly across the foyer to the stairs. He bounded up them, taking them two at a time.

After he left, the only noise in the room was the continued assault of the storm outside which filled Maggie with a curdling sense of foreboding.

Dead to Rights

L aurent paused at the landing at the top of the stairs.

Despite what he'd indicated to Maggie, while he didn't think the sound they'd heard was evidence of ghosts, neither did he think it was normal or just the sounds of an old house under attack by the weather. From where he stood, poised on the landing, the air felt still and silent all around him—as if the house itself was holding its breath, waiting for him. He stepped onto the hall carpet runner and heard the accompanying creak of the wooden floorboards beneath his feet.

He figured the sound they'd heard had been right about where he was standing now, at the head of the stairs. He flicked on his cellphone's flashlight beam and raked the walls of the hall with it.

The first bedroom then, he decided. He held his breath to better hear even the smallest sound as he stepped to the door, his hand hovering over the handle.

That's when he heard a soft rustling, like the sound of blankets being flapped or straightened out. Someone was in the room. He hesitated a moment longer before slowly pushing the door open.

Inside, the air was heavy with the scent of old wood and musty linens. The room was dimly lit by a single flickering candle which cast murky shadows on the walls. As his eyes adjusted to the lighting, Laurent could make out a large four-poster bed in the center of the room.

A figure was lying motionless on the bed.

Laurent quickly scanned the rest of the room with his flashlight but could see no other place for anyone to hide. There was only the bed, a nightstand, a dresser, a wash basin and an ewer. He turned his focus back to the bed and took a silent step toward it.

The figure was turned away from him, a coverlet on top. Laurent felt a tightening in his chest as he pulled back the covers. His fingers brushed against something cold and hard. He jerked back the covers and swore.

It was a skeleton. A full skeleton with arms, legs and skull intact. The bones were discolored, tinged in a shade that spoke of decades passed. Its skeletal hands rested on the outside of the coverlet as if patiently waiting for something...or someone.

When he jerked the covers, the skeleton's head had turned toward him. Its sockets, empty and hollow, gazed at him. Laurent took in a breath and let it out.

What was this thing doing here? Was the old woman actually insane?

Suddenly Laurent was aware of an odor of musty decay that seemed to permeate the entire room.

Something in the back of his brain reminded him of the reason he'd come here. The noise he'd heard. He glanced again around the room. But there was nothing here to explain the sounds. Slowly, without turning his back on the object in the bed, Laurent backed up toward the bedroom door, when suddenly he heard the soft creak of the door opening behind him.

Before he could turn around, a sudden explosion of pain ignited in the back of his head.

8

A Ghost Story

"Madame, no!" Maggie shouted as she lurched forward and grabbed the old woman's shoulder just as she brought the heavy trowel down on Laurent's shoulder.

Laurent staggered, then turned and shot out a hand and wrenched the gardening trowel out of the old woman's hand. Madame Lavallière whimpered in frustration.

"You leave him be! Don't you touch him! I'll kill you!" Madame Lavallière cried, as Maggie put a firm hand on her arm.

"Laurent, are you okay?" Maggie asked. She knew she'd stopped the woman from hitting him more than a glancing blow but it still had to hurt.

Maggie hadn't seen Madame Lavallière pick up the gardening trowel when, after asking where Laurent had gone, she had suddenly bolted across the living room to the stairs. As Maggie followed her up the stairs, Maggie had been trying to convince her that Laurent meant her no harm. She had no idea Madame Lavallière was going to attack him when she flung open the bedroom door and saw him in the room.

Maggie looked at Laurent where he stood by the bed.

"Laurent?"

"I am fine," Laurent said tightly.

He turned to Madame Lavallière and then pointed at the bed.

"Can you explain this?"

Maggie turned to look where he was pointing and let out a small gasp of surprise.

"Is...is that what I think it is?" she asked, reaching for Laurent.

The skeleton lay on its back, its hands on the cover, the empty sockets of its skull staring malevolently at her.

Dear Lord what have we walked into?

Madame Lavallière let out a single, broken-hearted wail and crumpled to the floor. Her thin arms hugged herself as tears streamed down her cheeks as she turned away.

"Don't touch him," she moaned through her tears. "He is my dearly beloved."

The wind howled outside, whipping the skeletal trees outside the windows into a frenzied dance, their branches scratching against the sides of the house as if clawing to gain entrance. Maggie shivered as she listened to the sound of the rain pounding against the roof in a relentless, drumming onslaught.

Around her, the flickering candlelight from three lone candles cast shadows that danced and writhed with each faint whiff of air that slipped through the cracks of the walls. They had all moved back downstairs to the parlor and now Maggie sat staring into what felt like the very heart of the storm raging outside. With every crash of thunder she felt the raw power of nature vibrating deep in her bones.

She turned to face Madame Lavallière who sat clutching a handkerchief and periodically dabbing her eyes. A shawl was wrapped around her shoulders as she stared down at the floor. Maggie had made more tea and found more cheese and brought that into the living room on a tray. Laurent was feeding the last of the wood into the fireplace.

Maggie felt she was still reeling from the shock of seeing the skeleton in the upstairs bedroom—a bedroom that was very clearly still being used, as evidenced by the frilly robe she'd seen at the end of the bed—by Madame Lavallière herself.

"Whenever you're ready, Madame Lavallière," Laurent said.

Madame Lavallière took a deep breath and seemed to gather herself in preparation for the story she was being forced to relate. Maggie saw the horror and reluctance in the old woman's eyes. As she began to speak, her words slow and measured, each word seemed to reveal a new depth of her pain.

"This villa belonged to my father's family for three generations," she said. "My brother and I lived here, and we were happy."

"It must have been quite something in its day," Maggie said.

Madame Lavallière looked at her and smiled.

"It was. When my grandparents were alive, it was grand. But when they passed, and my family moved in..." She sighed. "My father had troubles in the village. He was not the man my grandfather was. I think the village hated him for that. So, we lived here. Alone."

"What happened to your brother?" Laurent asked.

Maggie hadn't wanted to ask. She knew it was going to be a sad story. For a moment she wondered if that was the skeleton upstairs but no, Madame Lavallière was clearly sleeping with it. The skeleton wouldn't be her brother. At least she hoped not.

"He fell from the big apple tree in the far pasture," Madame Lavallière said. "We owned all the land then. Before my father sold it to pay for his debts."

Her voice quivered as tears cascaded down her face, threatening to consume all her energy.

"*Maman* was not the same after Nicolas died," she said. "I saw her give up. Even at ten years old, I knew she didn't want to live any longer."

Maggie couldn't imagine a young child having to understand such a dreadful thing. Her stomach clenched with sorrow at the burdens this poor woman had suffered as a child.

"I was twelve when she died," Madame Lavallière said. "By then, she had been sick for many months, and we all knew it was coming."

She looked up at Maggie and Laurent.

"But you are never prepared. Not if you love them. The war had just begun and with *Maman* gone, I thought Papa would lose his mind. He had not gone with the others when they were called but when the Germans came, he...left."

Maggie frowned.

"Left how?" she asked. "Was he taken prisoner?"

Madame Lavallière shook her head.

"My father was not a brave man. Not without *Maman*. He just ran."

"He left you here alone?" Laurent asked, incredulity and accusation thick in his voice. "Unprotected?"

Despite the sadness and pain that her story was causing her, Maggie could see there was a sense of strength and resilience in the old woman's voice. Maggie tried to imagine what it must have been like for a young girl to have been orphaned and left to live on her own in this huge house while the area came under Nazi occupation.

"How in the world did you survive?" Maggie asked.

"Well, one does," Madame Lavallière said with a sigh. "I had *Maman's* garden and the well."

"And nobody came from the village to see how you were doing?" Laurent asked.

"No. They hated Papa. For the longest time, I don't think they knew he'd gone."

Maggie caught Laurent's eye and he shook his head in disgust. She could see he was as moved and horrified by Madame Lavallière's story as she was.

"And the Germans didn't find you?" Maggie asked.

Madame Lavallière smiled then. But it was a bitter, cold smile.

"We are set far back into the woods," she said. "Even then we had no electricity, no telephone, unlike most people around here. A German officer came once, and when he saw how little there was, he never came back."

"I guess you were lucky," Maggie said. She could've bitten her tongue to have even suggested it after everything the poor woman had endured.

"Oh, yes, I was. After that, the bosch left me to myself. That is, until one day, just before my fourteenth birthday."

Madame Lavallière glanced at the ceiling in the direction of the bed with the skeleton and Maggie knew they were getting to his story now.

"A young German soldier came to my back door. He was hungry. I was surprised because normally the soldiers didn't come this far into the country. He had no rifle and he had straw in his hair. He had been sleeping in a barn. I knew immediately he had run away."

Madame Lavallière pulled her shawl tighter around her but now Maggie could sense she was warming to her story and to the memories of a time that had not been all bad.

"His name was Otto Himmelstein," she said, her eyes misting and a small half smile on her lips. "And yes, he had run away. I fed him and we talked, and he stayed. He said he had no family back in Germany and no place to run to and so he stayed with me."

Her eyes sparkled as she spoke, her voice soft and wistful now.

"I knew he was the enemy, but he was also the man I was made to be with. It wasn't our fault that the war happened."

She clasped her hands together, as if attempting to hold tight to the memories of her beloved. As she continued, describing her memories of the man who had captured her heart so many years ago, Maggie could feel the warmth and tenderness emanate from her. She spoke of the plans the two of them had made, of their determination to build a life together—the war couldn't last forever—the family they would create.

The old woman sat silently for a moment staring off into space as she imagined these happy plans. It was obvious to Maggie that the memories of their time together must have been the happiest moments of her life.

Laurent cleared his throat and Maggie glanced at him. He raised an eyebrow and glanced at the bedroom overhead, reminding Maggie that they still hadn't gotten the story of how the skeleton—clearly Otto himself—had gotten there. As if she'd interpreted Laurent and Maggie's silent exchange, Madame Lavallière shifted in her chair and continued.

"One night," she said, her voice flat and emotionless, "some villagers came to my door. I had been in the shops that day. I'd traded eggs for tobacco. We had chickens then. By then they knew that Papa was gone. And they became suspicious."

"What happened?" Laurent asked gently.

Madame Lavallière shifted again in her chair, suddenly uncomfortable and Maggie wondered if was really necessary to hear the story. What difference did it make? Whatever had happened was eighty years in the past and to make the poor woman relive it seemed suddenly torturous for no real reason.

"Somehow they knew Otto was here," she said, her voice devoid of emotion. "There were three. They came and they took him. One man held me in the kitchen. The other two..."

She swallowed hard and stood up as if too agitated to sit still.

"They killed him," she finished.

The awful words seemed to fall out of her mouth like stones dropping onto sand. Abrupt, thudding, insensate. In the silence that followed, Maggie was again aware of the sound of the grandfather clock in the hallway ticking away the minutes.

"So you...put him in the bed upstairs?" Maggie asked tentatively.

Madame Lavallière whirled on her, her face flushed with pain but also anger.

"I loved him! He came to me for refuge, and it was my people who killed him."

She sat back down on the chair and covered her face with her hands.

"He was the only man who ever loved me. And I couldn't save him."

Maggie moved to sit next to her and put an arm around her.

"I'm sorry, Madame Lavallière," she said. "War brings out the worst in some people."

"And makes heroes of others," Madame Lavallière said, sniffing and wiping away her tears. "My Otto was a credit to his people...If he had been allowed to live."

Maggie glanced at Laurent. It was truly amazing to think that this woman had lived with her love's corpse for nearly eighty years, and nobody had ever known.

"Didn't the villagers ever wonder about...why they never saw you?" she asked.

"After they killed him," Madame Lavallière said angrily, "they knew not to knock on my door."

That may be so, Maggie thought. But she could only imagine how hard it must have been to live the last eighty years alone with only grief and hatred to sustain you.

You might well go mad.

Suddenly, Madame Lavallière looked up at them. Her gaze which before had been steady and certain was now hesitant and suspicious. Maggie saw her lips were trembling.

"You won't tell, will you? If you do, they'll take him away. Please. Promise me you won't tell anyone about Otto."

"We won't tell," Maggie said, giving her shoulders a squeeze. "I promise.

9

Said the Spider to the Fly

L ater, after eating the cheese and also some sliced apples that Maggie found in the kitchen, Madame Lavallière insisted that Maggie and Laurent take one of the upstairs bedrooms for the night. The storm was still raging and there was no way anyone was going to be able to get word to anyone tonight. Reluctantly, they agreed.

"Take any room," Madame Lavallière said. "Except of course Otto's room."

Maggie felt a shiver of cold air at hearing those words, as if someone had opened an air conditioning vent somewhere in the house—which of course was impossible. She and Laurent retired upstairs, giving Otto's room a wide berth in the hallway, and chose one of the bedrooms at the back of the house. Like downstairs, the bedroom felt as if it had been frozen in time, with old, ornate furniture covered in a thick layer of dust. The room had a set of floor to ceiling windows that showed the full fury of the storm outside.

Laurent found a candle and a box of matches on the dresser where the old woman had indicated they would be. He lit the candle. Maggie thought she detected a faint whiff of dampness, as if the room has been exposed to years of moisture and humidity—and also something sour, like old food or rotting vegetation.

"You shouldn't have promised her," Laurent said as he sat on the bed, testing its springs. "Of course we must report the corpse."

Maggie sat down next to him, suddenly very tired. "Why?"

"*Chérie*, the soldier has a family back in Germany. They will have been wondering what happened to him."

"But it's been so long. Eighty years. Who is alive to wonder about him?"

"That is not the point, *chérie*. It is not up to you. They need to know what happened to him.

"I'm sure they figured he died in the war, which is true."

"You won't convince me not to tell the police. As I said, you should not have promised."

Maggie couldn't help but think of all the *other* things that Laurent had no trouble keeping from the police. She thought he could have made an allowance for this. However, as with everything that she didn't understand about Laurent, she imagined there was something in his past that was making him feel strongly about this now.

"I just thought that after everything she'd endured," Maggie said as she pulled back the coverlet on the bed, "that she should be allowed to live in peace."

Just then, Maggie thought she detected a subtle change in the light in the room. When she looked around she saw nothing to account for it and assumed it must be the flickering candlelight playing tricks on her eyes. As she climbed onto the antique four-poster bed, she was very aware of the wind howling against the bedroom windows. She'd have preferred to keep the candle burning all night but was afraid of burning the place down.

As soon as Laurent got in bed and pulled the coarse wool blanket over them, he drew her into his arms. Maggie loved sleeping like this, especially on a cold, rainy night, to hear the thump-thump of his heart as she lay her cheek against his chest. She knew that even if the place was brimming with unhappy spirits, at the end of the day, if Laurent was with her she was safe.

She yawned and was surprised to realize that she was actually sleepy. But she had no sooner closed her eyes when she heard a faint tapping on the door.

Laurent was up instantly. He opened the door, revealing Madame Lavallière in the hallway with a candle.

"I hate to ask you, Monsieur," she said tremulously. "But I fear I have heard a sound in the basement. I'm sure it is only rats but I'm afraid I have an old woman's nightmares and I cannot rest until—"

"I will go," Laurent said, turning to put his shoes back on. He hesitated in the hall. "Will you wait here?"

"Yes, Monsieur," she said. "I will wait here with your wife."

Laurent nodded, and disappeared down the hall.

Despite the fact that she was not alone, Maggie felt suddenly vulnerable, as if her world has suddenly become a hostile and unfamiliar place. One moment she was wrapped in her husband's loving arms feeling cozy and safe and the next, she felt as if she'd just done a free fall out of an airplane.

She stood next to the bed and something about the way Madame Lavallière turned to look at her made Maggie think for one terrible moment that she and Laurent had just stepped into a very carefully laid trap.

10

The Bitter Truth

Laurent pulled out his cellphone to access the flashlight as he hurried down the stairs to the main floor and then through the kitchen where he'd earlier spotted a door that he knew would take him to the basement. As he approached, he felt the hair on the back of his neck standing on end.

He pushed open the door, and was instantly hit with a wave of cold, musty air clawing up from below. It was pitch black. He probed the gloom with his light, but it only aided in illuminating less than a foot in front of him. He carefully descended the creaky stairs to the basement. Enclosed by stone walls and no windows, the sounds of the storm were cut off as soon as he entered the basement stairwell. He kept one hand on the single wooden banister that guided him down, mindful that the steps might be damaged or broken.

When he reached the bottom floor, he used his flashlight to inspect the space around him. The air was thick in his nostrils with the scent of damp earth and old wood.

The basement was one large room that seemed to span the width and length of the entire villa. Laurent was surprised. Normally these old *caves* were broken up to accommodate wine cellars or coal repositories. He felt a sense of unease creep up his spine.

He stepped further into the basement and as he played his flashlight beam along the floor and walls he saw that the room was filled with old furniture and broken bits of farming machinery—the kind that would've used a horse or oxen—all covered in thick blankets of cobwebs and rust. An ancient furnace was set in the center of the room. It was nearly November, and the house upstairs was cold. But this furnace clearly hadn't been used in decades.

He ran his flashlight beam up the wall to the ceiling where it connected with the floor joists of the first floor. The walls were made of rough, mismatched boards, stained black by centuries of water damage.

Heavy chains hung from the ceiling. Old bottles were scattered about, and the floor was covered with a layer of rubble, dirt and rat droppings.

A tower of ceiling-high shelves made of rotting wood held stacks of boxes containing decades-old clothing, shoe boxes full of faded pictures and yellowed crumbled papers.

As he moved deeper into the basement, Laurent's sense of unease grew stronger. He had always depended on this extra sense, an uncanny ability to sense or see certain things invisible to the human eye or even events that hadn't happened yet. It wasn't exactly extrasensory perception, but there were many times this special sense had literally saved his life. Other times, merely from apprehension by the authorities. In any case, he respected it. Tonight, he felt it crawling up and down his arms as it warred with the feeling of despair that was thick in the air.

Of course there were rats down here. There were rats everywhere in every *mas* in Provence. There were even rats in Domaine St-Buvard. Laurent had only intended to humor a nervous old woman. He'd done his due diligence. It was freezing down here.

Suddenly, he stopped, his heart racing in his chest. There was something unseen but without question there. Something malevolent. He approached the furthest corner of the basement, the beam from his flashlight strafing the floor and wall. At first he wasn't sure what he was seeing. But the presence of a bony femur jutting out from the mound soon made it clear.

It was a grave. Protruding from it were two skeletons half-buried, laying just a few feet from each other, their bones yellowed and brittle with age.

Three skeletons in one night. Maggie is getting her spooky Halloween after all.

He knelt to examine them. One skeleton had a knife in its ribs and the other a bullet hole in its skull. They were both dressed in homespun and baggy denim—clothes from another era. Could these be the villagers who had killed her German soldier? Laurent ran his flashlight beam along the two skeletons.

It was a gruesome thought but after what he'd heard tonight, he couldn't blame her if that's what happened. He frowned as he contemplated their mortal wounds. She would've had to have gotten close to kill the one with the knife. Had she stabbed him and then shot the other when he saw what was happening? Why had no one from the village come looking for them?

He sighed and got to his feet. He felt sure the authorities would be lenient with the old woman because of her age and mental condition. The skeletons were perfectly preserved, despite the passage of time.

The air in the basement seemed to grow heavier and more oppressive after his grisly discovery, and Laurent felt a sudden urgency to get back upstairs. For a moment he actually felt difficulty breathing. He glanced around. There was no telling what kind of toxic ventilation down here he was breathing. He glanced once more at the skeletons, his eyes fixed on their empty sockets. Before turning to go back upstairs he gave the area another rake of his flashlight beam and when he did, his eye caught something that made him hesitate. For a moment he only stared, not able to instantly compute what he was seeing.

All at once he was struck with the realization that Maggie was upstairs alone—with a serial killer. He turned and bounded for the stairs taking the steps two at a time, hearing them groan and give under his weight. The door at the top of the stairs was shut.

He was sure he'd left it open.

He grabbed the handle and pulled hard. But it was locked.

11

One Wrong Move

Maggie's heart raced as the kindly old woman who had given them tea and shelter for the night now sat in front of her staring daggers at her and emanating suspicion and loathing. Maggie tried to understand the cause of Madame Lavallière's altered demeanor.

She had been so kind and helpful up until this moment. But now, unmistakably, there was something rancorous lurking in her eyes.

"Your man killed Otto," Madame Lavallière said.

At first, Maggie didn't comprehend what she was saying. "My...?"

"I knew I recognized him," Madame Lavallière said, nodding her head. "You were with him that day, weren't you? When they came for my Otto."

Maggie realized that Madame Lavallière believed that she and Laurent had been the villagers who had killed her

German soldier! The maliciousness in the old woman's eye nearly made Maggie gasp.

"Madame Lavallière, that's not true," she said. "Laurent and I weren't even born then."

That was truly an idiotic thing to say to someone who was insane, Maggie thought, furious with herself. If Madame Lavallière really believed that she and Laurent had something to do with killing her soldier, telling her that she'd not been born yet was hardly a defense!

Without taking her malevolent gaze off Maggie, Madame Lavallière reached into her robe. Maggie was positive she was searching for a tissue or handkerchief. But instead, the old woman pulled out what looked like an antique pistol and aimed it at her.

Maggie's breath caught in her throat at the sight of the gun. Her hands started to shake with the adrenaline pumping through her, and she forced herself not to jump up from the bed.

She stared down the barrel of the gun pointed at her. She saw the loathing and anger in the old woman's eyes. Maggie had been a fool to think Madame Lavallière was just a tragic old lady with a sad story.

How did I ever think that someone living with a corpse for eighty years was normal?

Laurent was right. They needed to tell the police. Maggie licked her lips. She felt her anxiety trembling across her skin.

"Look, Madame Lavallière, I'm your friend. I promise."

Maggie knew that one wrong move—one wrong word— could mean the end of everything. Her breath seemed to hitch in her throat, and she felt her skin prickle with sweat.

"You're not my friend!" Madame Lavallière said. "You killed Otto. You killed the sweetest most gentle creature on this earth." Tears streamed down her face. "And now you are going to feel what *he* felt the moment nobody showed *him* any mercy."

"You're wrong, Madame Lavallière," Maggie said putting her hands up as if she could somehow protect herself from the bullets. "It wasn't us who hurt Otto."

Her mind raced trying to think of what might make the old woman believe her.

"That's what the last ones said," Madame Lavallière said as she raised the gun to Maggie's chest. "And they were lying too."

Suddenly Maggie heard a noise coming from what sounded like far below them. A steady pounding and a man's shout.

Laurent!

Maggie felt her pulse quicken with her mounting panic.

"What did you do to him?" she asked. "You led him into a trap."

Madame Lavallière smiled coldly.

"He is getting what he deserves. He pretended to be my friend, but he wasn't."

"I told you, we're working with the Resistance. With the Allies. We're on your side."

Madame Lavallière looked at her uncertainly.

"You are not with the Allies," Madame Lavallière said.

"What are you talking about?" Maggie said. "Can't you hear my American accent?"

"You're trying to trick me. The Americans aren't in the war!"

"We are! We...it just happened," Maggie said. "Don't you have a wireless radio? You'd have heard. We're in the war. You and I are allies, Madame Lavallière."

The older woman tilted her as if trying to understand Maggie more clearly.

"How do I know you're telling the truth?" she asked.

"You know Clark Gable, don't you?"

Madame Lavallière's eyes widened. "From the movies?"

"Yes, that's right. Well, Clark Gable is working with us—unofficially, of course."

"I don't believe you."

But her eyes told Maggie she *wanted* to, her expression told her that with just another little push, she would believe her.

"I understand you're scared and upset," Maggie said trying to maintain eye contact and speaking in a soothing tone, in spite of the panic fluttering in her chest. "You've done an amazing job for the Resistance all on your own. Your father will be so proud of you."

Madame Lavallière's eyes filled with tears and the gun sagged so that it was no longer pointed at Maggie's chest.

"We're not your enemies," Maggie said. "We're just two people who got lost on a stormy night and ended up here."

"Like the Allied pilot," Madame Lavallière said uncertainly.

"Yes, exactly. And you helped get him home, right?"

Madame Lavallière's eyes glanced in the direction of the basement for a moment and then she swallowed hard.

"I tried," she said. "But he made so much noise."

Maggie decided not to press that topic any further.

"I can see you're in a lot of pain," Maggie said. "Whatever happened to you in the past, it doesn't have to define what happens now. If you put the gun down, we can help each other. We can win this war together."

Suddenly a veil of suspicion enveloped the old woman's face, and she repositioned her gun on Maggie.

"That's what you would say," she said, "if you were trying to trick me."

Maggie heard Laurent continue to shout and she tried to remain calm, tried to imagine what was happening to him that he couldn't handle himself. Laurent was a big man who'd been in the kind of life and death scrapes that most people only read about.

"Okay, fine," Maggie said, seeing visions of a Hail Mary forming in her brain and trying to avoid making any sudden movements that might provoke the old woman into action. "I was hoping not to have to say this because it could get me in trouble with my superiors."

Madame Lavallière narrowed her eyes.

"Laurent and I are a part of a high-level advance team sent by Charles de Gaulle to assess the threat situation in this area."

"General de Gaulle?"

"Yes. He's coming over from London—secretly—to take the lead on this assignment."

Madame Lavallière frowned. "What assignment?"

"Assimilating intelligence in this area," Maggie said. "Bringing down Vichy and finding those embedded in the community who are working with the Nazi's."

Maggie knew that last gambit was a risk. If Madame Lavallière herself was one of those, it would be all the more reason to kill Maggie.

"General de Gaulle is coming here?" Madame Lavallière asked.

Maggie nodded.

"If my husband and I report back that your villa is an ideal headquarters for him, then yes, he will be coming here."

Maggie watched the old woman digest the information,

her eyes darting wildly around as if trying to see where the lie was. A loud crash sounded from below and then silence. Maggie didn't think she could wait much longer. Madame Lavallière repositioned the gun at Maggie's chest.

"Not just de Gaulle," Maggie said, taking in a fortifying breath, and getting ready for the Hail Mary. "But Otto Himmelstein, too."

12

Hell to Pay

Madame Lavallière stared at Maggie in astonishment, her jaw dropped open.

"What are you saying?" she whispered.

"I don't know who you think you...have in that bedroom," Maggie said, "but Otto Himmelstein is alive."

Madame Lavallière's eyes, which had moments ago burned with distrust and anger, now filled with tears of confusion and joy.

"But...but I saw him die!" she said.

"*Did* you? Someone died that night. But it wasn't Otto."

Maggie hated how she was creating this look of hope and euphoria on the woman's face.

"But...how?" Madame Lavallière asked, biting her lip.

"The night the villagers came for your German soldier was the same night the Resistance was doing a routine patrol of the area. Our intelligence told us that the villagers were going to raid your place and kill the soldier—who was working for us."

Madame Lavallière looked at Maggie with wonder and hope glittering in her eyes.

"But Otto never told me," she murmured.

"He was under orders not to," Maggie said. "You said you didn't see him killed, right?"

Madame Lavallière shook her head.

"They held me in the kitchen until it was over."

"And when they left, you came outside?"

Madame Lavallière was trembling now.

"They buried his body in the garden."

Maggie knew it was a wild shot, but she couldn't wait much longer. If she couldn't get the woman to give her the gun, she would have to make a grab for it and risk her pulling the trigger.

"And when did you...dig him up?" Maggie asked.

"I...I thought about it for a long time."

Madame Lavallière stood in agitation and began pulling at her hair. The gun fell to the floor with a thunk on the carpet.

"A week. And then I brought him to my...to..."

She looked at Maggie in horror.

"But then...who is in my bedroom?"

"It's a man named Wilhelm Schmidt," Maggie said, her mind racing to make the lie sound convincing. "He was a card-carrying Nazi. We found him planting a bomb under a bridge in Alsace where children walked to school. He was scheduled to be executed. But when Otto came to your villa and we heard of the planned attack by the villagers, our mission was to rescue him. When our men came, they fought with the villagers intending to kill Otto. During the scuffle they swapped the two men and escaped with Otto, alive."

Madame Lavallière let out a moan of rapture and Maggie hated herself for what she was doing.

"But...but...why?"

"They wanted the villagers to think they'd killed Otto so as not to alert the Gestapo in the area."

"But why didn't Otto write me? Why didn't he tell me he was alive?"

Maggie's mind raced.

"He couldn't. They...they shipped him to...to England. And...and he'd been hurt in the fight. He had amnesia."

"He didn't remember me?"

Madame Lavallière's joy which had been radiant just moments before seemed to evaporate, replaced by a rising expression of despair.

"Not until just recently," Maggie said. "He...he's waiting for you."

Madame Lavallière looked at Maggie in stunned wonder, her eyes once more bright with her mounting euphoria.

"And it's okay? For us to be together?" she asked, clasping her hands together in prayer and joy.

"Yes, it's okay. The war is almost over. You may be together now."

Madame Lavallière cried out in joy, then turned and bolted from the room. Maggie scooped up the gun and stuffed it under the mattress. Then she hurried down the stairs to the main floor and down the long hall, through the kitchen and to the door that led to the basement.

"Laurent!" she cried when she reached the door. "Can you hear me?"

She couldn't hear his answer, if there was one, because of the pounding of her heart in her ears. The door to the basement was latched shut.

"I'm here, Laurent!" she said as she struggled to lift the bolt, finally pulling it free of its box.

The door pushed open before she had a chance to touch the handle and Laurent stepped out, his face wet with perspiration in spite of the cold. He grabbed her arm and dragged her away from the basement door.

"Don't go down there," he said.

Maggie tried to remember the last time—if ever—she'd seen him so shaken.

"What is it?" she asked.

"There are two skeletons down there," he said.

Maggie was horrified.

"She told me an Allied pilot was staying with her," she said, looking down into the dark maw of the basement. "I got the impression from what she said that he didn't get out alive."

Laurent wiped the perspiration from his face and glanced at the ceiling. The sounds of footsteps moving overhead were loud and pronounced.

"Well, I didn't find the pilot but that's not to say he isn't down there," he said. "But that's not the worst of it. I think we might need to go back to the car tonight after all."

Suddenly Maggie felt as if a dark cloud had engulfed her. If Laurent was suggesting sleeping in the car in this storm, there must be something really horrible he wasn't telling her.

"What do you mean that's not the worst of it?" she asked.

He ran a hand up her arm and Maggie could tell he didn't want to upset her.

"Tell me, Laurent," she said firmly. "I don't want to have to go down there and see for myself."

"I would not allow you to do that."

"Then, tell me."

"There's another body," he said finally.

"Okay."

"Not a skeleton."

Maggie swallowed hard. "Oh."

"He's wearing Adidas and has a cellphone on him."

13

It Ends as It Begins

Maggie eyed the basement door with mounting anxiety. What did it mean that there were bodies down there?

Laurent pulled her away from the door and guided her through to the kitchen where they both stood for a moment as the storm continued to lash the windows and doors. One of the windows in the kitchen was broken and the rainwater poured in onto the wooden floor.

Maggie sat on one of the kitchen chairs, not sure if her legs would hold her for much longer.

"She held me at gunpoint," she said. "She made it sound as if she'd locked you in the basement."

"But how could she, if she was with you the whole time?"

"I don't know."

Maggie rubbed the goosebumps off her bare arms.

"She also made it sound as if she'd gotten revenge on the villagers who'd killed her German soldier."

Laurent nodded grimly.

"That would make sense of the two skeletons I found," he said. "But not the body."

Maggie shivered.

"What is going on, Laurent?"

"I don't know, but the body looks as if it's been there for a bit. I was thinking he might be one of the vineyard workers from last summer who left one day and never came back—not even for his pay. I took a few pictures on my cellphone."

Maggie shivered.

"I think she heard us talking about going to the police," she said. "I bet that's why she came and lured you to the basement with that story about rats."

"Where is she now?"

"I don't know. I lied to her and told her Hans was still alive."

Laurent's eyebrows shot up.

"Did she believe you?"

"I think so. It was all I could think of to distract her from the idea of shooting me! And it worked. She dropped the gun and ran out of the room."

"We don't know that she doesn't have other weapons," Laurent said. "We need to find her."

Maggie looked out the broken window at the storm raging outside.

"If she went outside…" she said.

"She wouldn't be that crazy."

"I don't know, Laurent. She's pretty crazy."

"We need to find her," Laurent said again. "We can't take the chance that she's not hiding somewhere ready to ambush us. In the morning, we will go for the police."

Maggie knew what he said made sense. Even as hard as it was pouring outside, the thought of spending the night here went against every natural instinct she had. She stood up and rubbed her arms again.

"Okay," she said. "Let's find her."

As they moved silently from the kitchen to the darkened parlor, using their cellphone flashlights to see by, Maggie couldn't help but feel a sense of turmoil deep inside her. The very air in the villa seemed thicker and heavier than before. The parlor itself was unnaturally quiet, like a tomb. The only sound was that of the wind blowing against the front windowpanes.

There were a few embers left in the fireplace, providing a glow of light besides their cellphone beams. Everywhere she looked, Maggie expected to see the old woman crouching, ready to jump out at her. But instead, only shadows lurked in the corners while eerie creaks echoed off the walls.

"Maybe we could stay here in the parlor?" she suggested. "And take turns standing guard?" She glanced at the stairs to the upstairs bedrooms. She really didn't want to go back up there.

"We need to find her," Laurent said firmly.

Maggie really wished there was a way they could simply barricade the bottom of the stairs to prevent the woman from getting out so that they didn't have to go up there and find her.

"She could have a whole armory of weapons," Maggie said.

"Where's the gun she had?"

Maggie turned to him in horror.

"I hid it in the mattress. Why are you asking about that? Laurent, we can't shoot her!"

"We can if it's her or us," he said grimly. "Stay in the living room."

"No way! I am not splitting up again!"

"Okay, fine. Stay close then."

He reached for her hand and led the way to the staircase. The entire villa seemed to creak and moan with every step as they crept up the staircase. Maggie heard a strange, muffled thud that seemed to come from the upper bedrooms. She held tightly to Laurent's hand until they reached the top of the stairs. There they stopped and took a breath.

"Are you ready?" Laurent asked as he moved toward the first door on the right, the one with Otto's skeleton in it.

"Are you sure?" Maggie whispered. "That's where she... that's where..."

Laurent didn't answer but positioned her behind him and then reached out and turned the handle on the door.

"Be careful," Maggie said as she imagined the door suddenly exploding in a splintering fireball as Madame Lavallière shot at them from within.

Laurent gave the door a gentle push. It swung open slowly, and he took a step across the threshold and peered inside the room. Maggie felt him stiffen and she moved out from behind him, too impatient to wait. Inside, a cold needle of air came from some hidden source accompanied by a strange musty smell.

Maggie played the beam of her flashlight into the interior. She could just make out the large four-poster bed in the corner.

The skeleton was lying motionlessly on the bed as before but now Maggie saw the shock of white hair on the pillow. She felt a tremble of dread race through her.

"Laurent?" she said softly. "Is it her?"

She could feel Laurent looking around the room, but

Maggie's eyes were glued to the sight in front of her. She could not look away. She walked over to the bed.

Madame Lavallière lay motionless on the bed. She was embracing the skeleton, her face pressed against its skull, her eyes closed as if in slumber. Maggie reached out and put a hand on Madame Lavallière's forehead. She wasn't yet cold but there was a sense of stillness and emptiness to her that told Maggie she was dead.

14

Darkest Before the Dawn

Maggie looked around the room, searching for a sign of what might have caused Madame Lavallière's death. As she scanned the room she noticed a bureau against the wall, its surface filled with old framed photographs of a life long gone. Children, parents, grandparents.

"What happened, do you think?" she asked, suddenly convinced that it was her tall tales earlier that had killed the old woman.

"Stop it, *chérie*," Laurent said, as if reading her mind. "You did not do this."

"But why tonight of all nights?"

"She is where she wanted to be," Laurent said. "Leave it."

On the nightstand by the bed was a drinking glass. It was empty but Maggie wondered if there had been something in it. Had Madame Lavallière poisoned herself? Why now?

Laurent pulled Maggie from the room, but Maggie was

glad to leave. The space was a somber and melancholy one. *However* the old woman had died, Laurent was right, one way or the other it was what she'd chosen.

They both went downstairs to the parlor. Maggie didn't have the stomach to stay in any of the bedrooms upstairs and the further away from the two bodies, the better.

Downstairs, Laurent lit the few remaining candles which immediately cast eerie shadows against the old wall-papered walls. He found some old tablecloths in the kitchen that he used to create a pallet for the two of them in front of the fireplace even though the fire was almost out.

"We'll ride out the storm," he said. "In the morning, we'll walk until we can get cell service."

The storm continued to batter the villa, the sound of the rain pounding against the windows added to Maggie's now definite sense of unease. After hearing about what was in the basement—and now with Madame Lavallière's death—the villa seemed to be virtually throbbing with dangerous mysteries. She sat and gazed around the parlor. If there was any other option besides staying here tonight, she would gladly have jumped at it.

Because the villa hadn't been updated or changed in over a hundred years, there was a definite sense of history to the place and especially this room. But as she sat here with the storm pounding all around her, all Maggie could think of was the lonely child living here for years trying to fend for herself surrounded by actual monsters.

"I don't think I can sleep," she said.

"Just close your eyes," Laurent said as he settled down beside her.

She lay down on the couch and pulled one of the heavy brocade tablecloths over her.

"I can't believe how she must have lived all those years,"

she said. "I can't believe the villagers didn't know she was here."

"Go to sleep, *chérie*. For her, it is over. And for us as well. We will be sheltered tonight and walk out tomorrow to find a cellphone signal."

Maggie listened to the storm batter the windows of the parlor. It seemed impossible to believe that the storm would finally be over tomorrow. It sounded as if it would never stop.

"I can't believe she died," she said. "Tonight, of all nights. Do you think she took something? Like an overdose? But why would she? I'd just told her that Otto was waiting for her. Does that make sense?"

"I don't know, *chérie*."

Laurent sounded tired and Maggie turned to look at him. He wasn't arguing with her, but she could see he was thinking. Something was bothering him. She watched him for a moment, the candlelight—sputtering now as the candles came down to their nubs—was reflecting off his face. His expression was troubled.

"How did you get locked in?" she asked.

"*Comment*?" He turned to look at her.

"When you were trapped in the basement."

"The door automatically locked behind me."

But Maggie knew he didn't believe that.

"The latch was dropped," she said. "When I opened it, I had to pull the latch up."

She saw a muscle flinch in his jaw.

"Laurent? How did the door lock behind you? Madame Lavallière was upstairs with me."

"It is a...loose end," he said.

Maggie felt a chill at his words. What was he saying? Was there someone else in the house? Was it ghosts?

"Laurent?"

"Maggie, go to sleep. In the morning we will—"

Suddenly, from somewhere in the house a music box started playing. Maggie felt her arms crawl with goosebumps.

"Laurent," she said, her voice laced with fear.

"There is a logical answer," he said.

"Like what?"

"I do not know."

Maggie sat straight up, straining to hear as the music played from somewhere in the house. The more she listened, the more uncomfortable she felt. Suddenly the idea of being here with Madame Lavallière dead upstairs and another body in the basement and two skeletons was becoming quickly unendurable.

"Do you think there are more?" she asked in a low voice.

"More bodies? I don't know."

Maggie felt her heart fluttering in her chest, and she tried to calm herself. "How did she kill...the one you think worked for us?"

"I saw no marks on the body. Perhaps she poisoned him. Or just lured him to the basement and left him to die."

Maggie swallowed hard.

"How about the two skeletons?"

"One stabbed. One shot."

Maggie took in a long breath to steady herself.

"She said there was an Allied pilot, too," she said. "It didn't sound like he made it out alive either."

"I don't know, *chérie*. I didn't look around that well."

The sound of a door slowly creaking broke into their conversation. Maggie felt as if she was about to jump out of her skin. Her flesh vibrated in fear.

"It is probably just the house," Laurent said, his eyes

going up the stairs as if he didn't believe his own words. "After so many years, it is uneven on its foundation. The doors will open of their own accord."

"Laurent, I don't like this."

The door slammed shut in an explosive sound and Maggie jumped to her feet. If there *were* spirits in the house, she imagined those spirits were probably very unhappy about now.

If spirits can slam a door, what else can they do?

Laurent stood up and headed for the stairs.

"Laurent, no!" Maggie screamed.

"Don't be *ridicule*, Maggie. There are no ghosts up there."

But he didn't sound as if he believed his own words. The sound of the slamming doors seemed to ripple up and down the stairs as if an unseen hand was slamming them one after the other.

"I'm sure that's all there *is* up there!" Maggie said. "Do *not* leave me down here!"

"I will not be a minute. I'm just going to see—"

Suddenly the doors stopped slamming.

"It heard you," she whispered.

"Don't be ridiculous."

But he said it without conviction. And he didn't go upstairs. Maggie studied his face. Even *he* knew the doors stopping right then was cause and effect. She held her breath for several long moments, but the house was quiet after that.

But it was not empty. Of that Maggie was sure. There was a presence in the house aside from themselves. It felt to her like a rock dropped into a pool of water, its rippling movement starting in the bowels of the house and spreading outward through the villa and even into the storm and the surrounding forest. Maggie saw it in her mind as clearly as if she were watching a movie.

Laurent sat on the floor, leaning against the couch, his ankles crossed.

"Come, *chérie*," he said, reaching for her. "It's just a bad night. In the morning, it will all look fine."

She moved to sit next to him as he put an arm around her shoulders.

"I wish it were morning," she said.

"It will be before you know it," he said, kissing her and easing back into the couch. He closed his eyes.

In the end, it was the sight of him looking so relaxed that finally helped to ease the tension out of Maggie's shoulders. That, and the culmination of the stress and weariness of the constant terror she'd been feeling all evening. The exhaustion seemed to hit her all at once.

One moment she was watching Laurent sleep and wondering how he could be so relaxed, and the next minute she was asleep herself—dreaming a dark and treacherous dream.

The man appeared before her as solidly as if he were corporeal. But she knew she must be dreaming. She heard a moan that she recognized as her own as she watched the figure come closer and closer to where she and Laurent sat on the floor. The man's features began to assimilate but wouldn't gel to form a picture. But she recognized the German uniform.

And the knife in his hand.

Maggie gasped as she fought to claw her way out of the abyss of the nightmare. The closer he came, the harder she fought to awaken, until she heard her breath catching in desperate, frantic hiccoughs.

It was her own scream finally that woke her. She sat up,

her heart pounding in her chest, and turned to see Laurent who was still fast asleep.

Had she screamed? Or had she dreamed that too?

Turning away from Laurent she saw a faint light filtering through the window outside. A sense of dread began to build deep in her bones.

She shook her head violently to stay awake. But the pull of her exhaustion was too strong and she drifted off again. The next time she felt herself resurfacing she heard footsteps, a soft shuffling sound, like someone moving stealthily across the room. She opened her eyes and squinted into the darkness. There she saw the shadows move and fluctuate and morph once more into the figure of a man.

His uniform was torn, his arms and legs seeming to sprout from the clothing openings unnaturally—like an ogre forced into human clothing. He himself was transparent and ethereal. His hair was blond, his eyes fixed on her, as if he was trying to communicate with her.

Maggie shook her head, a jolt of fear and disbelief galvanizing her into full consciousness as she stared at the apparition in front of her.

It's real.

It stood in front of her, wavering. Watching. She stared back in horror until it slowly shifted its gaze from her to Laurent.

She saw the hand with the knife raise up. And she began to scream.

15

A Wing and a Prayer

L aurent's eyes flew open at the sound of Maggie's scream.

He saw the shadow looming over him, the blade glinting in the guttering candlelight. He rolled away at the last instant. But the shadow stepped closer, his arm finishing its downward arc toward his chest.

Instinctively, Laurent shot a forearm out to block the attack then drove his free hand upward to grab the wrist of the attacker's knife hand. He twisted it sharply. The attacker howled and Laurent heard the knife drop to the hardwood floor.

Out of the corner of his eye, Laurent saw Maggie. She was too close.

"Get back!" he commanded her.

"Laurent, he—" Maggie started to say.

In a sudden burst of movement, the man lunged again, using his weight to try and overpower Laurent on the floor. Laurent pulled his fist back to slam it into his attacker's face.

But something was wrong. He felt his adrenaline pumping, his muscles straining with the effort to hold back from striking him.

"*Nicht Kampf!*" Maggie shouted suddenly.

The attacker stopped, his wrists now both trapped in Laurent's hands. He turned to look at Maggie.

Then Laurent saw what he'd only guessed at when he'd grabbed him. His ghostly attacker was indeed real. And very, very old. Laurent dropped the man's wrists and climbed to his feet.

The man was dressed in a German uniform that no longer fit him. He looked alternately at Laurent and then Maggie, his expression one of both hope and sorrow.

"*Mutti?*" he whimpered.

16

Come the Dawn

T he first rays of daylight began to filter through the tall parlor windows a few hours after the storm had finally passed. Maggie awoke and disentangled herself from the covers on the floor. She saw Laurent standing in the open door looking out onto the front drive. She wasn't sure he had ever gone back to sleep after the attack.

Herman—their elderly assailant—was asleep on the couch. Laurent had debated tying him up, but in the end decided he was harmless enough.

"The rain has stopped," Laurent said as Maggie got to her feet and straightened out her clothes.

Beyond where he stood in the open door, Maggie could see the trees still dripping with water. The long winding driveway was muddy and broken up by patches of weeds. The air was heavy with the scent of damp earth and fresh rain. She stepped out onto the veranda with Laurent, blinking in the bright morning light and then turned to look back into the living room where Herman still slept.

"What do you think will happen to him?" she asked.

Laurent glanced over his shoulder at the man snoring on the parlor couch.

"He won't be able to stay here," he said.

"Do you think he'll be okay?"

Laurent ran a hand down Maggie's back and smiled at her.

"He will be fine, *chérie*. Probably for the first time in his life."

After he'd attempted to scare them away last night, Herman had broken down and told his story—as a child might tell it after a bad nightmare. He had lived his entire life in the villa—just he and his mother—and had been taught to fear and mistrust anyone coming to the villa. He lived in a little shed in the back garden and only come to the villa last night to find his mother because the storm had frightened him. He'd admitted to locking Laurent in the basement.

While he'd stopped asking for his mother and was happy to eat the meal of hot tea and cheese and apples that Maggie made for him, Herman was clearly very confused about who they were and why they were in the house. Eventually, Laurent convinced him that he wouldn't be harmed and the old fellow—in his late seventies—finally curled up on the couch and fell asleep.

"Are you sure you'll be okay?" Maggie asked Laurent as she pulled on a heavy jacket she'd found in the hall closet.

"We will be fine," Laurent said. "I'll make Monsieur Herman more tea. Just walk until you get cell reception."

"I will."

"Call the police first and then Grace. She and Danielle will be very worried."

"I won't be long," Maggie said.

Even as much as she hated to leave Laurent, she physically could not wait to get clear of the house. She hurried off the veranda and down the long driveway to the road. With every step away from the house she felt stronger and more alive. When she reached the main road, she headed in the opposite direction of where they'd left the car since she knew there was no cell reception there. She hadn't walked a mile in the opposite direction before her phone connected.

She called the police first and briefly told the shocked dispatcher about the bodies in the old villa and gave directions as best she could.

"There have been some trees down after the storm," the woman said. "But I think we will come to you first."

After that, Maggie saw the fifty messages on her phone screen from Danielle and Grace.

"Maggie! What happened to you?" Grace gasped, answering her phone in a panic. "We have been beside ourselves all night!"

"We're fine," Maggie said. "I'll tell you all about it later. How was the party?"

"*What* party? When you didn't show, and you weren't answering your phone, I tried to drive around looking for you, but the weather was so bad I had to give up. We've been worried sick!"

Maggie knew their car would've been invisible due to the storm and the moonless night.

"Is Amelie okay?" she asked.

"Yes. We didn't tell her you guys were missing. Thank God you're okay."

After talking a few more minutes, they disconnected and

Maggie called a garage in Aix to have the car towed. By then she was already walking back to the villa. As she turned down the driveway, she saw a patrol car idling on the drive.

The *gendarme* stuck his head out the window.

"Are you the one who called?" he asked.

"Yes," Maggie said.

"Did I hear right that there are four bodies here?"

"Afraid so."

The cruiser drove on and parked in front of the veranda. Maggie saw Laurent open the door and step outside. The policeman met him on the veranda and spoke to him before going inside. Laurent waited until Maggie reached the porch to give her a quick hug before joining the *gendarme* in the house.

17

One Week Later

Maggie was sitting on the couch in the living room at Domaine St-Buvard with a glass of wine in front of her and a cashmere throw across her knees. The crackle and pop of the burning logs and the heat radiating from the fireplace seemed to wrap the room in a blanket of warmth, warding off the outside night's chill. Grace and Danielle sat opposite her in two overstuffed chairs on either side of the fireplace. They had come for dinner at Domaine St-Buvard for a much needed evening of fellowship and friendship.

The scent of burning wood mingled with the faint aroma of baked apples and cinnamon from the kitchen. Laurent had made an apple tart for dessert that was its usual alchemy of sugar and pastry.

Laurent had cooked *choucroute garnie* tonight, and had then volunteered after dinner to take Grace's grandson

Philippe and Amelie, along with the two dogs to the village café to see if *chocolat chaud* was still in the offing. There had been an early frost last night and Laurent had been up at dawn checking on the vines. The area of Provence where they lived didn't usually get severe weather this soon in the season. In spite of the possible danger to their vineyard, Maggie felt a conflicting set of emotions at the sight of the frost.

On the one hand, nothing was more delightful than snuggling by the fire while looking out at a winter wonderland. On the other hand, she always thought there was something a little bit sad about the first real sign of winter. It meant the death of what was and the promise of a dormancy where nothing grew or flourished.

She shook the dark thought from her mind and focused on Grace and Danielle. The brief respite from dogs and grandchildren gave the three of them all a much needed chance to talk. It had been too long since they'd been able to fully catch up—and to finally debrief about that Halloween night a week ago.

When Maggie and Laurent had not turned up at the party or responded to their phones, Grace had immediately contacted the police who told her they hadn't been missing long enough for the police to do anything about it. Grace left the party and scoured the dark countryside on her own before the weather finally forced her to go home to wait and pray that her friends would turn up.

Maggie watched the twilight through the living room windows as it painted the landscape in hues of lavender and gold. Even shrouded in the soft twilight, the undulating landscape of the adjoining vineyard was still visible. The gnarled branches of the grapevines were coated in a delicate layer of ice-like brilliant sculptures.

She shivered at the sight and moved her hands closer to the fire. Laurent had built it up before he left and it roared merrily in the stone hearth, its flames casting a warm, flickering glow around the room.

"I still can't get over that the villa you stumbled upon was not even ten miles away from *Dormir*," Grace said, referring to the *gite* where she and Danielle lived. "And yet we never knew."

Maggie turned to Danielle. The older woman had lived in the area for three decades—longer than either Maggie or Grace.

"You really never heard anything about the family?" Maggie asked.

Danielle shook her head.

"No, nothing, *chérie*. Madame Lavallière stayed well-hidden."

"I still can't believe she lived there alone with her child all those years," Grace said, shaking her head.

From what Maggie had learned from the social worker who'd come later that morning to take Herman to a facility where he would be cared for in his remaining years, he had been raised alone by his mother, never having left the villa. He apparently suffered from a mild intellectual disability.

"Were they able to identify the two skeletons in the basement?" Danielle asked.

"Ah yes, and there's been an update," Maggie said. "One more skeleton was found in the garden."

"Good Lord," Grace said. "What happened?"

"Well, it seems that the skeletons in the basement were the men from the village. There's no clue as to how they got there other than my own theory which is that Madame Lavallière lured them back to her place either separately or together."

"Planning on killing them?" Danielle asked.

Maggie shrugged.

"The coroner said the two were killed at least sixty years ago, so Laurent and I think they were revenge killings."

"What about the poor man who'd worked Laurent's vineyard the summer before last?" Grace asked.

"He probably just got too close to the house, maybe came by asking for water or something to eat," Maggie said. "I imagine she got him down to the basement on some pretext and locked him in where he died of thirst and starvation."

"You said there was another skeleton?" Danielle asked.

"Yes. A British pilot."

Danielle made a clucking noise of dismay.

"I don't know what happened to him," Maggie said. "He might have been wounded and just died naturally when he didn't get medical attention. I remember Madame Lavallière saying he made a lot of noise."

"Oh, that's gruesome!" Grace said. "What a horrible woman!"

"It's no defense for what she did," Maggie said. "But I keep reminding myself that she was abandoned by her parents when she was eleven years old."

"How old was she, do you think?" Grace asked.

"Ninety-one."

"And how old was her son?"

"Seventy-eight."

"So he's definitely the son of the German soldier who was killed? Otto?"

"Well, no one's doing a DNA test, but presumably. He thinks he is, anyway."

"How did the village not know these two were there all these years?" Danielle asked, shaking her head.

"Nobody even knew Valène Lavallière was pregnant," Maggie said. "She rarely came to town. And Herman, either."

"He seriously lived to be seventy-eight years old without ever stepping outside the grounds of the villa?" Grace asked shaking her head in disbelief.

"Looks like it."

"What about property taxes?" Danielle asked. "Even if Madame Lavallière owned the place outright…"

"I think all that just fell through the cracks during the war. Madame Lavallière's father never returned from wherever he spent the war…"

"Probably killed one way or the other," Danielle said.

"Probably," Maggie agreed. "And the family had always pretty much kept to themselves."

"So Madame Lavallière just kept on living there. How?" Grace asked.

"She had a garden and a well."

"Pretty bleak. Although I suppose in a way it *was* a love story."

"A pretty tragic one," Maggie said. "Especially for anyone who had the misfortune to come into contact with her."

"You and Laurent included."

"Still, as spooky stories go, it was a pretty epic way to spend Halloween," Maggie said with a laugh. "I came *this* close to getting Laurent to admit he believed in ghosts!"

They laughed and as they did Maggie remembered that moment when she and Laurent were in the upstairs bedroom talking about going to talk to the police after discovering Otto when she thought the light had changed in the room.

Laurent told her later that one of the detectives said

they'd discovered a peephole attached to the adjacent bedroom. Madame Lavallière had obviously been watching them. That's why she came to lure Laurent to the basement. She'd obviously heard them talking about reporting her and Otto.

Maggie took a sip of her wine and nestled further into her cozy nest of cashmere, allowing herself to feel the delight of being snug and warm inside her home on a cold November evening.

"Well, it sounds as if it was an extraordinary experience for both of you," Danielle said.

"It was," Maggie said. "I'm not saying I believe in ghosts or anything, but there were a few moments there when I wasn't too sure."

"Yes, but it sounds like in the end there was an explanation for everything," Grace said.

"There was," Maggie said hesitantly. "Everything except when the music box started up on its own."

"Stop it, Maggie!" Grace admonished. "You're giving me goosebumps."

Maggie laughed and then felt another surge of well-being as she heard Laurent and the children come into the house.

"Well," she said with a smile, "after all, isn't being scared the whole point of Halloween?"

"No, darling," Grace said. "The whole point of Halloween is dressing up in costumes. And next year, we're going to the party in my car. And I'll drive."

Maggie laughed. "Sounds like a plan," she said.

Just then, Laurent came into the room.

"Everything good?" he asked, looking around the room as the two children bounded in and settled onto the couch next to Maggie.

She put an arm around each of them and smiled at Laurent.

"Pretty much as good as it gets," she said. "Just as soon as you trade in that old Peugeot for one that's less than a decade old."

He raised an eyebrow but also gave a slow nod that she chose to interpret as meaning that, whatever unforeseen adventure happened *next* Halloween, it would not be because of a stalled car.

ABOUT THE AUTHOR

USA TODAY Bestselling Author Susan Kiernan-Lewis is the author of *The Maggie Newberry Mysteries,* the post-apocalyptic thriller series *The Irish End Games, The Mia Kazmaroff Mysteries, The Stranded in Provence Mysteries, The Claire Baskerville Mysteries,* and *The Savannah Time Travel Mysteries.*

Visit www.susankiernanlewis.com or follow Author Susan Kiernan-Lewis on Facebook.

Books by Susan Kiernan-Lewis
The Maggie Newberry Mysteries
Murder in the South of France
Murder à la Carte
Murder in Provence
Murder in Paris
Murder in Aix
Murder in Nice
Murder in the Latin Quarter
Murder in the Abbey
Murder in the Bistro

Murder in Cannes
Murder in Grenoble
Murder in the Vineyard
Murder in Arles
Murder in Marseille
Murder in St-Rémy
Murder à la Mode
Murder in Avignon
Murder in the Lavender
Murder in Mont St-Michel
Murder in the Village
Murder in St-Tropez
Murder in Grasse
Murder in Monaco
Murder in Montmartre
Murder in the Villa
A Provençal Christmas: A Short Story
A Thanksgiving in Provence
Laurent's Kitchen

The Claire Baskerville Mysteries
Déjà Dead
Death by Cliché
Dying to be French
Ménage à Murder
Killing it in Paris
Murder Flambé
Deadly Faux Pas
Toujours Dead
Murder in the Christmas Market
Deadly Adieu
Murdering Madeleine
Murder Carte Blanche

Death à la Drumstick

The Savannah Time Travel Mysteries
Killing Time in Georgia
Scarlett Must Die

The Stranded in Provence Mysteries
Parlez-Vous Murder?
Crime and Croissants
Accent on Murder
A Bad Éclair Day
Croak, Monsieur!
Death du Jour
Murder Très Gauche
Wined and Died
Murder, Voila!
A French Country Christmas
Fromage to Eternity

The Irish End Games
Free Falling
Going Gone
Heading Home
Blind Sided
Rising Tides
Cold Comfort
Never Never
Wit's End
Dead On
White Out
Black Out
End Game

The Mia Kazmaroff Mysteries

Reckless

Shameless

Breathless

Heartless

Clueless

Ruthless

Ella Out of Time

Swept Away

Carried Away

Stolen Away

Printed in Great Britain
by Amazon

29583129R00054